Three Together

igloo

igloo

Published in 2008
by Igloo Books Ltd
Cottage Farm,
Sywell,
NN6 0BJ
www.igloo-books.com

10 9 8 7 6 5 4 3 2 1

ISBN: 978 1 84561 931 2

Cover design by Insight Design
Cover illustrated by © Rachel Ellen Designs Ltd
Interior illustrations by Liz and Kate Pope

Printed and manufactured in China

The Mystery of the Reluctant Pony

by Carol Lawrence

igloo

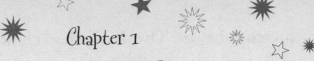

Chapter 1

Into the Wild

Sam grinned. His tongue and teeth were covered in brown shiny gunk.

"Arghghh," he growled making his vampire face at his big sister Poppy and her best friend KC.

"Sam, you're gross!" said Poppy. "Chocolate spread and peanut butter mixed together. Yuck!"

Seven-and-a-half year old Sam was always eating strange combinations of food.

"Mmm, neat," said Sam, munching.

Poppy gazed happily around the holiday cabin that was to be their home for the next two weeks. It had been designed in the style of an early American settler's shack, with imitation fur rugs, rustic furniture and a mock log fire with a rocking chair on one side.

The lights were disguised as old-fashioned lanterns that could be switched on with the flick of a switch. The dishwasher and refrigerator were tucked away behind the slatted wooden doors of a pretend-dresser. The dresser had china hooks and shelves displaying simple, homely crockery.

"It really feels as if we're out in the wilderness, doesn't it?" sighed Poppy.

"Even better than that!" exclaimed Sam. "I can use the laptop. The signal's great."

Poppy smiled, "Typical! Sam, you should get out more."

"Whatever," said Sam. Sam was computer-mad.

"Why don't you come pony riding with us, Sam? It'll be great," KC prompted.

"No way! Not on one of those things," Sam frowned, grabbed another slice of bread and coated it in peanut butter.

"But that's what this holiday centre is for," said Poppy. "Pony riding."

"No way," Sam replied. "If I want to go riding then I'll just play my Crazy Cross Country computer game."

KC stacked the plates into the dishwasher. "You don't know what you're missing," she warned.

"Oh, yes, I do. I'm missing a sore bottom, that's what," Sam replied, between finger licks.

Suddenly, KC's mum flew into the kitchen carrying her medical bag. "Come on you three, let's go. We've got a pony going down."

"What does that mean?" asked KC, puzzled.

"There's a pony over at the stables that refuses to be ridden. It keeps dropping to the floor when anyone attempts to saddle it. But that's all I know yet, KC," said her mum.

"Perhaps there's a pony strike," suggested Sam.

"Well, Sam, it's certainly a mystery," said KC's mum.

Poppy and KC flashed an excited look at one another. They snatched up their jackets and were waiting outside the cabin door before KC's mum could say a word. There was nothing the friends liked more than solving mysteries!

As they hurried towards the stables, KC felt very proud. Her mum had studied to pass the exams for a place at the local veterinary training practice. She had done so well that she had been selected to shadow Ruth, the most experienced vet at the holiday centre.

When her mum told KC the news, KC was very happy. But, KC was even more thrilled when her mum said that her best friend Poppy and Poppy's younger brother, Sam, could come to the holiday centre, too.

KC's mum quickly walked down the woodland track towards the pony centre with Sam and the girls chatting merrily behind. They jumped over the stile and strode out across the meadow; the stables were a ten-minute march from the woodland cabins.

When they reached the stables, Ruth was waiting for them in a stable block, beside the strange little Welsh mountain pony called Dixie. Kim, the stable manager, was smoothing the pony and talking to him with soothing words.

The three friends' chatter faded as they approached the stable door and peered over the top.

"We've got a mystery here," said Ruth to KC's mum. "He won't have anything on his back. As soon as we try, Dixie goes down like a lead weight."

Poppy, KC and Sam stared adoringly at the pretty pony. KC gasped at how sweet he looked. "He's so small and cuddly," she said.

"I hope he didn't hear that," said Sam, disgusted.

Kim sighed, "He's small, but don't be fooled. Dixie's a strong one."

Dixie was chestnut brown with a pretty biscuit-coloured mane. His wide set hazel eyes were alert and bright.

Kim was brushing him down and keeping him calm.

"He looks healthy enough," said KC's mum, checking his teeth and nostrils.

Ruth agreed. "He is, and there's no sign of ill-treatment on his back, either; no markings at all."

The pony shook his head and pulled towards Sam, Poppy and KC as they leaned over the door.

The girls reached out to him, but Dixie nuzzled and sniffed Sam's hands with his flared nostrils. Suddenly, he snorted and blasted a loud, wet sneeze all over Sam.

"Urgh! That's gross!" moaned Sam, wiping his wet hands on his jacket. "Smelly horse." Poppy and KC laughed.

"Why don't you three keep Dixie busy, while we check him over?" suggested Ruth, quickly.

Sam was making funny faces at Dixie while Poppy and KC leaned in closer and smoothed the pony's nose. Ruth walked around him, checking his fetlocks and belly.

"OK," said Ruth. "Let's try to put a blanket on Dixie's back."

KC's mum unfolded a speckled horse blanket and tossed it across to Kim, who caught it, and then they gently lowered it onto Dixie's back.

As soon as Dixie felt his back being

covered, he went down onto his knees, then his back legs and, finally, lay on his side on the stable floor.

"No, Dixie," puffed Kim, trying hard to pull him back up by the leather harness. But Dixie was too strong and stubborn. He just would not budge. Dixie's eyes were twinkling and he seemed to be looking mischievously up at Sam and the girls.

"That's weird," said KC.

"Maybe he doesn't like the colour of the blanket," said Sam.

KC chuckled and Sam flushed. "Well, I've got a jumper Mum tries to make me wear. It's got snowballs and mountains on it. It's awful," he moaned. "I'd rather wear Dixie's blanket."

"Maybe he's just used to being ridden bareback," suggested Poppy.

"No, Poppy . . . it's not the blanket or even the saddle. He won't allow any weight on his back and most certainly not a rider," said KC's mum.

"I've only just bought him from Bay Tree Farm," said Kim, who was feeling a little disheartened. "If he won't be ridden, I'll have to sell him."

Poppy and KC's ears pricked up. They didn't want Dixie to be sold without at least having tried to solve the mystery of why Dixie wouldn't allow a rider on his back.

"Is Bay Tree Farm near here?" Poppy asked, excitedly.

Kim looked surprised. "It's just down the road."

Ruth smiled knowingly, "He can't go back to Bay Tree Farm. Ponies aren't exchangeable like shop goods. If a pony won't co-operate after you've bought it, it's your problem, I'm afraid."

"Not in my Crazy Cross Country game," said Sam triumphantly. "In that game, I could even exchange Dixie for an elephant."

"I don't think we'd squeeze an elephant in here, Sam," said Kim, patiently.

KC's mum could see what was running through the girls' minds. "Looks like we've got two detectives onto the Dixie case," she said.

Poppy and KC nodded.

"Three detectives," saluted Sam.

"You'll be the officer in charge, no doubt," said

KC's mum, with a chuckle. Sam grinned.

Poppy was deep in thought. She decided there was only one thing to do; they'd have to visit Dixie's previous home to investigate his past and try to discover why he wouldn't be ridden. Poppy wondered what could have happened to make Dixie behave in such a strange way.

Sam beamed excitedly. "I'm going to do some research on my laptop. I might learn something about daft ponies."

"Good idea!" said Poppy.

"We'll see you back at the cabin," added KC.

Sam hopped down and walked warily across the stable yard. All sorts of ponies were leaning out of their stables watching him as he crossed the yard.

There was a small, chubby, white-headed foal with its nose stuck in the air, straining to see over the high stable door. Next to it was a tall, dark, fiery-eyed horse, just like Sam thought a knight in shining armour would ride. It was snorting and puffing, almost like a dragon, and shaking its head at Sam.

Until then, Sam didn't realise just how

different horses were. "They're just like people," he thought. He decided that he would be the fiery dragon horse and Poppy and KC would be the quirky little ponies. Sam was relieved that the ponies on his computer game were so tiny and easy to control. He'd even jumped the Grand Canyon on a silver steed on level five of Champion Rider without any problem at all. The ponies surrounding and watching Sam from the stable blocks were very different from his game ponies.

The girls watched Kim coax Dixie back up onto his feet. KC's mum and Ruth tried lowering the blanket over his back again but he went down once more. First his front legs, then his back legs, then he lay down on his side.

"Oh, Dixie, what are we going to do with you?" asked Kim.

Poppy hopped down from the stable door with KC close behind her. "Guess where we're going?" said Poppy, excitedly.

"Bay Tree Farm?" replied KC. They hadn't been friends all this time for nothing!

Poppy laughed. "Let's go!"

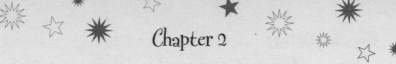

Chapter 2

Friend or Foe?

Poppy and KC shot around the corner of the stable yard and came to a sudden halt. An Arab horse reared up in front of them, coming back down to earth with a mighty clash of hooves, only to lurch up again.

Poppy and KC gasped in shock and backed up against the stable wall, trying somehow to merge into the stone.

"Whoa, steady, steady!" growled a tall, willowy girl. She was confidently yanking at the reins, trying to pull the Arab back down to the ground.

The Arab was scuffling and jumpy, but the girl skillfully tugged and inched in the leather rein until the horse's head was low enough for her to grab by the jowls.

She growled sternly at the stallion as she drew it obediently to her.

"Gosh, sorry we scared it," blurted KC.

"It? He's not an 'It'. He's called Chancer," said

the girl, flatly.

"It, um, I mean Chancer. He's the biggest horse I've ever seen," said Poppy, nervously.

The girl frowned at Poppy and KC.

"Not regular stable hands, are you?" she asked, dismissively. "There are lots of signs saying 'no running'. Can't you two read?"

KC was a little shocked by the girl's rudeness. "Sorry, we didn't mean to cause a problem. The horse was just there."

The girl sniggered. "Of course the horse was just there. You're in a stable yard! You half-scared Chancer to death."

"Me? Scared the horse? I was terrified," said KC.

Poppy could see KC getting angry, and decided to cool things down. "After all," Poppy thought, "it was a stupid thing for them both to do."

"You're right," Poppy interrupted. "We should have been much more careful. It's our first morning here. We've only just come up from the holiday cabins in the woods."

"Oh, holiday makers. They're the worst,"

muttered the girl, with contempt.

KC was blushing red with anger and looked ready to burst. Poppy thought she could almost see steam coming out of KC's ears.

"We are really sorry about scaring Chancer," said Poppy, apologetically.

The girl was surprised by Poppy's friendly response.

"Oh, right! Well. No real harm done, I suppose," she said, stroking the neck of the trembling horse.

The girl flicked her very long ponytail off one shoulder and frowned.

"Anyway," started KC, "I'm perfectly capable of reading. Just because . . ."

But KC fell silent when she saw the girl inspecting the horse. The girl dragged her right leg clumsily behind her as she walked round him. Her brow was furrowed and she was obviously very self-conscious and uncomfortable.

KC suddenly felt very badly.

It was obvious that the girl had a problem walking, so it would have taken a lot of effort for her to the calm such a big horse down.

"Um, I was saying," said KC, "I haven't had a chance to read the signs round here. I'll have to catch up on those later."

"Can we help? Is there anything we can do?" asked Poppy.

The girl's eyes suddenly flashed angrily. "Look, just because I've got a limp doesn't mean I need you to help, OK? I was riding horses before I could walk and, just in case you hadn't noticed, I can walk," she said, offended.

Poppy was shocked by the girl's attack.

"S-s-sorry," mumbled Poppy.

But the girl had already tugged on the horse, muttering, "Come on, Chancer," as she limped away, angrily.

"Great!" grumbled Poppy. "What an amazing start to making new friends here. "

KC shrugged. "Yes, it's hardly as if anyone was badly hurt."

"That's just it. I really upset her," said Poppy.

"You were just trying to be helpful. Anyone else would have realised that," said KC.

But Poppy wasn't convinced.

"Anyway, remember? We've got a mystery to solve. So let's stay focused," said KC.

Poppy's face suddenly came to life. "You're right. We can at least try to help Dixie," she said, with a sparkle in her eyes. "We need to discover what's going on."

This time, the girls walked calmly back across the stable yard. But once they'd jumped over the stile and were out in the open fields, they dashed along at breakneck speed, relishing their freedom in their exciting new surroundings.

Ten minutes later, they both burst breathless and panting into the cabin, looking for Sam.

They heard him shouting at the computer.

"Must be near the end of another level," observed KC.

"Well, we'd better wait until he's finished it before we ask him to find Bay Tree Farm for us on the internet or he'll be grumpy for the rest of the day," said Poppy, with a giggle.

Suddenly they heard another voice. It was a stranger's voice.

The stranger shouted cheerfully. "No way Samson, I don't believe it, you computer wizard."

Poppy and KC crept up and tapped on Sam's door.

"Busy!" Sam called.

"Can we come in?" asked Poppy.

"Hey, Samson, don't be mean," said the stranger.

"Well, OK," agreed Sam, "But watch the screen because I'm winning – wey hey!"

Poppy and KC peeked curiously round the door.

Sam was sitting cross-legged on the floor with his back to them. Another boy, with light brown hair and a friendly face, was sitting on the low cabin bed, wildly pressing the joystick buttons.

"Hi," said Poppy.

"Yes!" said Sam, tapping the buttons on his joystick. "Got you now, my friend."

There was a strange clanging sound and the picture of a metal grill shooting down from a castle doorway came onto Sam's screen.

"Ah, well done, Samson. That's ace," said the stranger, in defeat. "I've never been beaten at that game before."

"It's just practice," said Sam, proudly.

"Sam's had too much of it, if you ask me!" said Poppy smiling.

"Meet my new friend – Nathan," said Sam hopping to his feet with a bow. "Nathan's eight-and-a-half," he continued, impressed.

"Well, nearly," said Nathan, awkwardly.

"What happened at the stable?" asked Sam.

"We've got a problem pony," KC explained to Nathan. "It won't wear a saddle."

"That sounds strange," said Nathan.

"It's another mystery for us to solve. We can always do with an extra detective," said Poppy. "Are you interested?"

"Detective?" asked Nathan, happily. "That sounds great! Count me in."

Sam beamed.

"We need to find out where Bay Tree Farm is," said Poppy. "It's around here somewhere. Can you look on the internet?"

"On the case," said Sam quickly, as he shut down the computer game.

"Bay Tree Farm? I think I know where it is. I can take you there," said Nathan.

"Great!" exclaimed Poppy. "Kim at the stables bought the pony called Dixie from Bay Tree. But we need to find out why he keeps going down onto the ground. And we need to find out what set it all off. Bay Tree Farm is a good place to start."

"Let's go," said Sam, playfully pushing Nathan towards the door.

Poppy had a strange feeling that this holiday was going to be their most exciting yet.

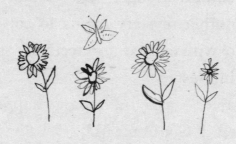

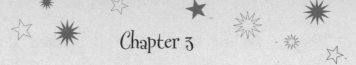

Chapter 3
Hiding Out

The group of young detectives cut through the woodland and came out at the main road that led into town. They found themselves in a small suburb that ran opposite the lane up to the stables and the adjoining fields. Houses ran back up a steep hill and sloped off into the distance.

"There's a great indoor pool near the shopping centre," said Nathan, pointing towards the hypermarket signs, "but that's about a twenty minute walk into town."

"We've got our own tour guide!" said Sam.

"But if we do go swimming," continued Nathan, "I'll have to bring my little sister Kylie. She wouldn't let me go without her."

"How old is she?" said KC.

"Five. My dad's on his own now, so he hasn't got a lot of time to do things like that with us anymore. He's getting his business started. He makes wooden toys. They're really neat."

"Wow! What kind of toys?" asked Poppy, impressed.

"Puppets, mainly. Puppets on strings. His business is called Gepetto Puppets," said Nathan proudly.

"I might call you Pinocchio then," said Sam.

"No way," said Nathan, "Or I'll make you play football with Kylie. She's an evil kicker. She always lands one on my shins."

Everyone laughed.

As the group walked past town on their way to Bay Tree, Poppy wondered just how they were going to help Dixie. If they could at least find out what was making Dixie fall to the ground in such a strange way, then KC's mum and Ruth might be able to help Dixie overcome it. But, although Poppy loved horses and was so looking forward to learning to ride on her holiday at the stables, she also realised just how little she knew about horses.

Poppy, KC and Sam soon discovered that the local town wasn't small. It had a cinema, an indoor leisure centre, a beautiful old church with a local museum at the side and a large park with a huge pond at one end.

Tall willow trees cast dark leafy reflections onto the water as the group chatted happily and crossed over the tiny stone park bridge.

"I think Bay Tree Farm is out past the industrial estate. I've never been there, but I've driven past the sign for it lots of times with Dad," said Nathan.

"You know what? I'm ready for peanut butter sandwiches," said Sam, his tummy making deep gurgling sounds.

"You can have some at my house on the way back, if you want," said Nathan.

"Can we see the puppets, too?" asked Poppy.

"Sure," Nathan said, lifting his palm.

"High five!" shouted Sam with a clap.

It was a long walk before they finally reached the roughly-painted road sign to Bay Tree Farm.

They walked up a long pot-holed track and came to the farm gate.

The gate had a lopsided sign on the front,

'Private property. Keep out.' Poppy hopped onto the steel tube gate bars and peered over with the others.

"So this is where Dixie came from," said Poppy with curiosity.

"Well, it looks pretty normal from the outside," KC announced.

Suddenly, Sam pointed at a small hill running up from the left of the farm. The hill was far away but the group could see another farm gate and what looked like a stile.

"What's that?" he asked.

"Cows," replied Nathan.

"No, they're not," said Poppy, "Look! They've got long skinny necks and tiny heads like camels. I really think they're camels."

KC strained over the gate and screwed up her eyes. "You're right. They are camels. What a strange place for a herd of camels."

"Cool," said Sam.

"Wicked!" said Nathan.

"Let's get a closer look," prompted Poppy.

"But we'll have to go past the farmhouse. That's

the only way through that gate," Sam said, with a worried note.

Suddenly, they heard the sound of a heavy engine and something rattling noisily up the bumpy track towards the gate.

"Quick! This way," said Nathan, diving over the gate and into the farm entrance.

Poppy, KC and Sam leapt over the gate after Nathan and followed him across the paddock.

"Where are we going?" cried Poppy.

"Where we can't be seen," called Nathan, as he raced ahead.

He headed towards the farmhouse and a low wall of hay-bales that were jutting out between the paddock and the farmyard.

Nathan dived behind the bales, closely followed by Poppy, KC and Sam.

The group sank down between the prickly bales and peered excitedly through the cracks.

"Ouch!" yelped Sam.

"Shhh," said Poppy.

"I've just been bitten," said Sam, indignantly.

"It's all that peanut butter Sam. It makes you

irresistible to ants," whispered Poppy.

KC and Nathan tried hard not to giggle.

"Whatever," Sam whispered, annoyed.

They all crouched down and watched. An old battered car towing a rusty trailer rolled up the farm track. It swerved to a halt in the cobbled yard right in front of the bales.

As the friends looked on, a sullen looking man got out of the battered car and slammed the door shut. He kept his head down and marched, hunched up and grumbling around to the back of the trailer.

With a clatter of chains and a loud bang, the trailer doors opened out from each side and a metal sheet crashed to the ground to create a platform.

There was a loud whinnying and, suddenly, a small grey and white dappled pony stumbled nervously about on the metal flooring of the trailer.

Poppy and KC gasped in shock at the pony before them.

Chapter 4
Cruel Beast

The pony looked as if it had been starved. The girls could count its ribs down each side of the pony's chest. Its black mane was clumped with dirt and, as it shook its head in fear, they could see the whites of its terrified eyes.

"Get on!" growled the man.

The man untied some rope from a bar inside the trailer.

The other end of the rope had been knotted around the pony's neck. The man tugged hard on the rope, "Get on, when you're told," he shouted, tugging on the fraying rope.

The man turned his head and spat at the cobblestones in frustration.

Terrified, the pony tried to back further up into the trailer. It lifted its head as high as it could and shook with fear.

Poppy was looking on in disgust. "I might not

know a lot about horses but that's not how you treat a pony," she whispered with contempt.

"Oh, Poppy, the poor thing is starved," KC muttered in shock.

"And terrified, too," added Poppy.

The pony fought against the pull of its tormentor.

Suddenly, the man pulled a long whip from the side of the trailer

"Think you're a mule do you?" he shouted, striking the pony with a lash.

Sam rose up and was about to jump out and shout at the man but Poppy pulled him back.

"No, Sam. It could be dangerous. We must stay hidden," she whispered.

"She's right, Samson, we have to keep our heads down," said Nathan.

"But, but I've got my camera, here," said Sam, angrily. "I need to get a picture."

"You can't – he'll see you. Just wait a second," said Poppy, calmly.

The pony took another lash of the whip to its

back legs and jumped halfway down the steel platform.

The man held the roped pony, then shoved it hard off the platform.

The pony whinnied and stumbled momentarily on the cobblestones before regaining its balance.

"Get on, you flea bag," hissed the man.

The pony stood, twitching and shaking in fear on the cobbles as the man lifted his boot and gave the pony a hard kick on its leg. The pony jumped and was then half dragged and half stumbled into an old broken barn opposite the farmhouse in the cobbled yard.

Moments later, the man reappeared from the barn. Sam peeped up from above the hay bales and clicked his camera; then he was down again within an instant.

The man kicked the barn door shut and tied it up tight to a wall nail, using the string he'd taken from around the pony's neck.

Then he stormed over to his trailer. As the man kicked up the platform and slammed the side shutters across, Sam snapped another photograph.

When the man started the old car engine, it roared a cloud of thick, black, spluttering smoke from its exhaust.

The man swerved the car and trailer back around and drove like a madman out of the farmyard.

"Quick, Sam!" said Poppy. "Take a picture of the number plate."

Quick as a flash, Sam had taken the photograph in seconds, and just before the car was out of range.

Poppy dug her hand into her jacket pocket and took out a tiny note pad and pen.

"I've got the registration plate," said KC.

Poppy looked at her watch and noted down the time.

"Can you remember what the man looked like?" asked Poppy. "We might need the description later on. It might help our investigation."

"Yes, I can – and there was a sticker on the side of his trailer," said KC quickly. "It was advertising Chillweld Farmers' Market."

"Brilliant!" exclaimed Poppy, eagerly scribbling down some notes. But when she turned back to Sam and Nathan, they had both disappeared.

Poppy nudged KC. "I bet I know where those two have gone," Poppy pointed towards the old barn.

They peeped out from behind the hay bales.

"Suppose someone's watching from the house?" whispered KC.

Suddenly, the distance between the hay bales and the back of the barn seemed as wide as the Grand Canyon.

Poppy's eyes lit up. "Think like a cat," she said, stretching her fingers like claws.

Then Poppy crept low down through the grass like a wild tiger and, KC had to admit, it looked pretty clever.

"OK," whispered KC to herself, "if I'm going to be a cat, I'm going to be KC the aristocat," and she followed Poppy silently along.

"You took your time!" Sam laughed, as Poppy and KC prowled around the barn wall and stood up beside him.

"You can't rush KC the aristocat," KC stated.

"What does the KC stand for?" asked Nathan.

"Don't even try to find out," replied Poppy. "It's the best kept secret in the world. Not even I know, and I've been KC's best friend for years!"

Nathan looked curiously at Sam. Sam just shrugged his shoulders innocently and gave a weak smile.

"OK," said Nathan, bending down and linking his fingers together. "Who's going to climb up and look in the window?"

Sam piped up, "It's obvious," as he pointed at Poppy.

Poppy beamed, and put her multi-coloured trainer on Nathan's cupped hands.

With Nathan's help, Poppy carefully hauled herself up to the edge of the crumbling stone wall.

"What can you see?" KC called, anxiously.

Sam got up on tiptoe but he was still way below the barn window.

"It's so dark, I can't thing a thing," moaned Poppy. "But I can hear something moving around."

34

Suddenly, they heard the wheels of a car on the cobbled yard at the front. Poppy balanced and wobbled on Nathan's now muddy hands but had to lean heavily on his head, too.

"D-d-don't worry about me," stuttered Nathan, "I'll just be shorter than my sister after this."

Sam chuckled.

"I think I can see the whites of the pony's eyes, but –" Poppy strained further in.

They heard the slam of a car door.

"We've got to go!" hissed KC, urgently.

Poppy rocked back and forth then jumped down onto the grass with a gentle thud.

"I couldn't see the pony, poor thing. I feel so sad for it," said Poppy.

"Me, too," agreed KC. "That man was cruel. Maybe that's why poor Dixie acts so strangely."

"But your mum said Dixie hadn't been hurt," said Poppy, puzzled. "And she would know. Well, there's got to be an answer and I'm sure this is where we'll find it."

They heard the slam of another door and the sound of growling, barking dogs on the other side of the barn.

"They're coming this way," said Sam, anxiously.

"Run for it!" cried Poppy.

"Time to disappear!" announced Nathan.

All four turned and dashed away from the barn. They raced into the small paddock where, at the far side, a small patch of trees offered safety and cover. Then they were halfway to the outer fencing when Nathan looked around.

"Don't look back. Just RUN!" cried Nathan.

Two huge, Great Danes were tearing towards the fleeing group.

The dogs were howling and barking wildly and, with every step, were closing in on them.

"I – I'm not going to make it!" gasped KC.

"Oh, yes, you will," said Poppy, and she grabbed

KC's hand and dragged her even faster through the field.

By now, Nathan and Sam had already cleared the fence.

They were hopping up and down on one of the fence panels like runners in a relay race waiting to grab the baton from the girls.

Poppy and KC lunged breathlessly at the fence.

"Watch out!" yelled Sam. He snapped off a dead overhanging branch and threw it at the attacking animals. The dogs sped off course momentarily and sniffed at the branch, then careered on towards Poppy and KC.

But Sam's branch tactic was just enough to distract the hungry animals for long enough while Poppy and KC leapt to safety over the high fence.

They could hear the rattle of mesh and the creaking of wood and knew that the hounds were standing up and clawing at the fence.

The four friends kept running. No one dared to look back as they stumbled on through the sparse woodland.

But, as the sound of barking grew fainter, they began to relax and slowed down to a gentle jog.

"I – I think . . " panted Nathan. "I think we'll be okay now."

KC halted, leaned over and rested down onto her throbbing knees.

"What are we going to do now?" asked Sam, collapsing onto the ground.

Poppy thought for a while, wondering what a detective would do next. Not just any detective of course, but a special detective – a fully trained and street-wise, fearless and clever detective, who was on a mission to save the lives of not one but two sad and helpless ponies.

"Well, you've got some photographs, Sam. We can show them to Mum and explain what we've seen today," said KC.

"I did get some, but none of the poor pony," replied Sam. The man would have seen me. I just got a couple of shots of the man and the car as he drove away."

"There's only one thing to do," mused Poppy. "We'll just have to go back. We need to get a picture of that poor pony, too. We need to find out what's being done to it so that we can help Dixie."

"Poor Dixie. But we can't go back now. We'll have to come back later when the dogs aren't around," agreed KC.

"She's right," said Sam. "Those dogs must have been bigger than the pony we saw. They'd have me for lunch no problem."

"Come on," Nathan piped up. "Let's go back home to my house for some sandwiches and you can meet my sister."

"Yes, then we can draw up a plan of action," said Sam, excitedly.

"Sounds great!" chorused Poppy and KC.

It suddenly looked to Poppy as if they were on the way to solving the mystery of Dixie after all – and they might even be able to help another pony in distress.

Chapter 5

Puppet on a String

As soon as Sam, Poppy and KC arrived at Nathan's house, they were grabbed by Nathan's little sister Kylie and dragged out into the garden.

Kylie chattered faster than a chipmunk and her brown ringlets bounced up and down with every word.

The five year old marched everyone into to a small greenhouse in their tiny garden and announced "This is my dad," in her most grown up voice.

Kylie and Nathan's dad was leaning over a carved puppet that had been carefully laid out on a small workbench.

Poppy and KC's eyes lit up.

The roof of the greenhouse had two long poles running from end to end and each pole had at least fifty puppets hanging from silver thread. As the sun beamed in through the old glass panes it warmed the room and illuminated the rich colours of the puppets.

Poppy took a deep breath. She could smell woodchip and paint, sunshine and damp grass. Wooden Russian dancers, Arabian princesses, Japanese Acrobats – even puppets of Romeo and Juliet – danced delicately from the transparent roof of the greenhouse.

Sam, Poppy and KC gulped in amazement at the feast of colours and assortment of characters that met their eyes.

"Wow, that's a white wizard from my Gate to the Lost World game!" exclaimed Sam.

Sam pointed at a wizard puppet hanging just above him and studied it.

"Have I got it right?" asked Nathan's dad with a smile.

"You bet!" exclaimed Sam looking at the puppet as if it were magic.

"Thanks. I've had an order for one hundred of those on a promotion for a gaming company. Good to know it's passed the ultimate test," said Nathan's dad.

Sam was awestruck.

"These puppets are incredible!" said Poppy, her eyes sweeping up across the sunlit ceiling.

"Yes, magic!" exclaimed KC, admiring a mahogany fox with a beautiful red bushy tail and a blue velvet waistcoat.

"Well, take a good look at them, kids, because I'm afraid I won't be making puppets like these for much longer," said Nathan's dad, flatly.

"Has the council decided not to let you stay and rent your workshop, Dad?" asked Nathan, anxiously.

"Afraid so, Nate. Someone else has got the workshop now and there's no way I can afford anywhere else. They bolted up the workshop before I even had the chance to get the rest of my carpentry kit back," said Nathan's dad.

"But . . . but the tools are yours; they belong to you. What are you going to do?" asked Nathan.

"Don't worry. I'll get into my old overalls and start working back at the garage," said Nathan's dad. "Anyway, this talk is for another time, Nathan, when we're alone. I've still got another fifty white wizards to make."

Nathan frowned.

"Cool," said Sam, "Your wizards are amazing."

"Thank you," smiled Nathan's dad.

"Footie!" yelped Kylie, dragging a reluctant Nathan and his friends from the greenhouse.

"Park only," Nathan's dad called after them. "I don't want a storm blowing through my greenhouse windows."

Nathan's face softened as he picked up Kylie and marched into the house. "Lunch first," he said, seating Kylie at the kitchen table.

"What's happened to your dad's workshop, Nathan?" asked Poppy. She could see Nathan was worried and wanted to help if she could.

"Forget it," said Nathan. "Dad's told me to."

After lunch and a dangerous game of football with Kylie, the three friends hobbled back through the woods and sank back into the comfort of the log cabin.

It had been a dramatic start to their holiday. They were all still reeling from their traumatic experience at Bay Tree Farm. But meeting Nathan and his family helped take the edge off of their sadness.

Poppy knew they all had a lot of detective work left to do if they were going to stop Dixie from being sold.

Chapter 6

A Lonely Prince

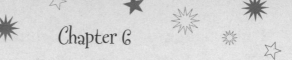

KC's mum was up early the next morning, singing along to the radio as she made breakfast.

"Come on, you three!" she called from the little kitchen. "Anyone would think you were on holiday."

Poppy peeped out from beneath her panda sleeping bag on the cabin bed. She looked across at KC who was still sleeping. KC still had all her pigtails in from the day before and one of them was sticking up in the air like a poodle's tail. Poppy giggled and threw her pillow at KC.

KC was awake in an instant and blasted Poppy's pillow back at her. Then KC hopped out of bed and gave a loud yawn and a stretch. "I had nightmares last night about the Hound of the Baskervilles," she confided to Poppy.

45

Poppy laughed, "I had nightmares too, but mine were about a mad footballer called Kicking Kylie." Poppy rubbed her bruised shins.

By the time Poppy and KC got to the table, Sam was already up and eating his cereal.

"Looks like you're in for a busy weekend," mused KC's mum. "We've all been invited to a birthday party."

"Wow! That sounds great!" said KC. "Whose birthday is it?"

"Not whose, but what?" replied her mum. "It's been ten years since Kim first opened Rocky Mountain riding stables, so she's going to have some anniversary celebrations over the weekend."

"Cool!" cheered KC.

"It will give you all the chance to meet the riders who work at the stables," continued her mum.

"We've already met one," said KC, thinking back to their collision with the girl with the limp and Chancer. "We didn't get off to a good start."

"Yes, but she had a very bad leg, KC, and we didn't make things easy for her," said Poppy.

"Oh! Sounds like you bumped into Phoebe,"

said KC's mum. "Was she a tall, slim girl with a blond ponytail almost down to her waist?"

"Yes, that's the one," answered Poppy.

"Well, KC, I'm surprised at you for being so ungracious. Phoebe's a lovely girl," said her mum.

"I didn't say I didn't like her. I just think she's difficult," said KC.

"Well, you would be difficult too, if you'd been through what she has. She was the stable's top rider until last year, when she had a terrible accident on her pony," said KC's mum.

KC looked at her mum. "Was that pony a great big, frightening beast called Chancer?"

Her mum laughed. "That was just the problem. Chancer is no monster. He is the biggest softie in the whole world. He gets startled very easily. Last year Phoebe took him out for a hack and something frightened him."

"Yes, I can believe it. He went wild when we ran past him in the stables," said Poppy.

KC nodded in agreement, remembering the earlier incident. "What happened to Phoebe?"

KC's mum sighed. "Poor Phoebe! She can't

remember very much about the accident. She heard the sound of a shotgun and Chancer took fright. Kim told me they only found out when Chancer came wandering back to the stables without Phoebe."

"That's scary," said Poppy.

"The stables organised a hunt and discovered Phoebe badly injured up near the old monument. They think she must have been dragged along by one of the stirrups because of her injuries; it was lucky she didn't lose her leg."

"That's tough," said Sam, deciding that pony riding was best done on his computer game.

"And things have been even tougher for Phoebe since the accident. She can't ride because her leg's too painful but she can't stay away from the horses, either. She just adores them. It's very sad."

"I get uptight if I can't play my computer game for an extra half an hour," agreed Sam. "But to never be able to play a computer game again?"

"Oh, Sam!" said Poppy, impatiently.

"But why doesn't she do something else? Maybe she could swim?" asked KC.

"Because that's what it's like when you love horses. You love everything about it, from the thrill of riding, to the relationship that you build up with your horse. Most of those girls at the stables would willingly live there twenty four hours a day, if they could, and Phoebe's no different. Kim has to kick them out and send them back home most evenings," said her mum.

"How sad," said Poppy, thinking about Phoebe, Dixie and the sad little pony, too.

"Life is hard sometimes. But I think Phoebe will be all right." KC's mum thought for a while, then said, "Though Kim's a little worried about her at the moment because she's very moody with her old friends at the stables. It's an odd mixture of the girls feeling guilty about still being able to ride when Phoebe can't and Phoebe feeling understandably jealous of them."

"I know!" exclaimed Poppy. "Let's ask Phoebe to come swimming with us next week."

"Yes, that's a good idea," agreed KC.

"Worth a try," said KC's mum. "If you can prise her away from Dixie, that is. She's building quite a bond with the strange little pony, which isn't good news as Kim will probably have to sell him soon. But, do try; it's a great idea."

Hearing this, Poppy's resolve to help Dixie became stronger than ever. "There has to be a solution to the problem," thought Poppy, "if only I can figure it out."

Later that day, Poppy, KC and Sam decided to go to Rocky Mountain Stables and offer to help with the party preparations. They knew KC's mum, Kim and Ruth would be busy checking on any mares in foal, so they guessed it was time for them to break the ice with the girls at the stables.

Poppy, KC and Sam had reluctantly agreed to meet Nathan after the weekend. They had wanted to go back to Bay Tree Farm earlier than Monday. But Nathan was desperate to join them on the mission and pleaded for them to wait for him. He couldn't go before then because of a "family thing" as he called it, which he couldn't get out of.

The three friends headed towards the meadow leading up to the back of the stables. Suddenly, they heard a horse neighing on the other side of the hedge. Moments later, the horse was leaning over the top of the hedge, pulling and chewing at the leaves. It seemed eager for some attention.

"What a beautiful horse!" exclaimed KC.

"Yes, it's pretty, um, nice," said Sam, resisting the urge to stroke it and be sneezed on again.

A little further up from the horse they found a small stone step linking the horse's field to their own. Sam sat down on the step, planning his next move on level eight of his game. KC and Poppy hopped over and went to see the horse.

The horse walked confidently up to them and nuzzled Poppy's jacket. It was so affectionate that

it almost knocked Poppy off of her feet. She giggled and stumbled back then stood by its side and patted it adoringly.

"What a fantastic colour it is," said KC.

The horse was brilliantly white on the head and body but had dappled black markings on its rump and lower legs.

Poppy laughed, "I think it's one of those special breeds, an apple oosh um, or an Arabian or something."

"I'd call it Apple, or Pip, or something like that. No, maybe Snowy or . . . " KC pondered for a moment.

"What do you think you're doing?" a voice demanded coldly from behind the girls.

Poppy and KC whirled around to see a young girl holding a riding crop.

She was red faced and frowning, her small nose puckered. She started tapping her riding crop menacingly on the palm of her hand.

"You're on private property," she said.

"Oh, we didn't realise; sorry. We just came in to see the horse," said Poppy, quickly.

"Well, now you've seen it, you can get out of my field," said the girl sharply. "And don't come near my horse again. Prince doesn't like strangers."

"We thought it was a Rocky Mountain stable pony," said KC quickly.

"You must be kidding!" said the girl, indignantly. "Prince in with those scrag ends? I might have had my lessons there, but that's the end of it. They're all hopeless. I've got my own private teacher, now."

"Well, I think Kim is lovely," Poppy announced, defensively.

"You're on private property. So I'll have to ask you to leave," retorted the girl.

"I don't see a sign or notice to say this is private property," continued Poppy "and that looks like a public entrance."

Poppy pointed to the stone step.

"Not for much longer, it isn't. My father's got friends on the council. He plans to close this whole field off to stop people like you wandering in," said Harriet Durston, for that's who she was. "And I can guess where you're from," she continued snidely, "Those disgusting old shacks in the woods."

"They're holiday cabins," said Poppy, angrily.

"Harriet suddenly stood between Prince and the two girls, but Prince had other ideas and he tried to nuzzle around Harriet for some more affection from the girls.

Suddenly, Harriet lifted her crop and stung Prince on the side of his neck.

Poppy and KC visibly winced at the sound and Prince dutifully backed off.

"Oh, that's awful!" exclaimed KC. "You don't deserve a rat, let alone a horse."

Harriet sniggered, "You probably don't know anything about either."

Poppy watched KC's face. She saw the red mists of anger brewing in KC's cheeks until she was fit to burst steam from her ears. Only this time, KC actually blew her top.

"Listen! Your horse looked lonely, so we came to show it some affection, if you know the meaning of the word! There's nothing clever about whipping a horse," shouted KC.

The girl was obviously not used to being challenged or insulted.

"I'll speak to my father about you," spat the girl, venomously. "Nobody speaks to Harriet Durston like that. My father runs half of the businesses around here and he won't have strangers talking to me like that."

Poppy could see the indignant tears misting in the girls cold blue eyes.

"Well, perhaps you should have been a little more polite," said KC, feeling much better after her outburst. She tapped Poppy on the shoulder. "Come on Poppy, we don't want to waste our precious time here," she snapped.

Poppy was embarrassed and upset at the same time. Suddenly, they heard Sam calling them, "Come on you two, we've got work to do." He was standing on the stone step, waving impatiently.

"I'll get you for trespassing," Harriet Durston called after them. "Just you wait."

Chapter 7

Party Ponies

"Great," said Poppy, as they marched on to the stables. "One enemy made in Phoebe, now another in that Harriet person."

"Well, I certainly wouldn't want that Harriet person as a friend," grouched KC, still slightly flushed from the meeting.

"I hope we don't bump into her again," grumbled Poppy. "The people around here are turning out to be mean, moody and rather rude."

"But ... what about Nathan?" asked Sam.

"Well, not him," said Poppy.

"And Ruth?" asked KC.

"No, not her," replied Poppy, quickly.

"And what about Kylie?" said Sam.

Poppy started to laugh, "No, not Kylie either."

"I suppose you think Kim's horrible, too, then," laughed KC, mischievously.

"All right, all right, maybe not everybody's mean," Poppy conceded, cheerful again.

The three marched out like the Musketeers – united and ready for adventure.

When they arrived at the stables it was busier than they had ever seen it before.

There were small groups of girls laughing and blowing up balloons.

A young boy with bright orange hair was holding a ladder steady while a girl was pinning a happy birthday sign across the top of two stable doors.

"Steady, Theo, I'm not an acrobat," commanded the girl.

"Um, whatever," grumbled the boy.

Sam nodded at him in sympathy.

Brightly coloured bunting blew gently around the doors of the tack rooms as the latest songs rang out of a radio into the yard.

A small marquee was set up on the green beside the stables. Inside the marquee, decorated tables had been set out and covered in white paper tablecloths in preparation for a feast.

Poppy suddenly erupted into laughter. One of the riders marched out of the tack room wearing fancy dress. The girl's face was covered in green paint. Her riding helmet had an assortment of bouncy springs with silver stars bobbing about on the top. She was wearing a number nine riding strip with 'Marsha the Martian' painted across her chest.

She beamed at Poppy and her friends.

"Wow! A friendly Martian," said Poppy.

"I knew we'd find a friendly face somewhere around here," KC remarked.

"Hey, anyone who comes to the party has to wear fancy dress," Marsha called out to them.

"No way!" protested Sam. "After all," he thought, "fancy dress is just not cool."

"Come on, Sam. You'll look great," said KC.

"No," he replied, stubbornly.

Poppy and KC dragged Sam over to the waiting Martian. The Martian held up a tub of face paints with a grin.

"No, don't!" said Sam wriggling and writhing between Poppy and KC.

But Poppy, KC and the Martian already had Sam trapped in the chair. Soon, Sam emerged shocked with a Spiderman web across his face.

"Cool!" said a group of girls dancing just outside.

"Yeah, whatever," said Sam sounding bored, but, once past the group of admiring girls, he grinned, happily.

"Looks like you've been rumbled," said Theo, the boy with bright ginger hair. He'd escaped his ladder duty because he was hopeless at it.

"Yes," agreed Sam, "A surprise attack."

"Hah," laughed Theo. "They haven't managed to hold me down long enough to get the paint on . . . yet!"

Ten minutes later, KC came out, displaying a beautiful butterfly face, closely followed by a tiger-striped Poppy.

"Rarr!" growled Poppy. "Let's party!"

One of the stable girls jumped onto another girl's back.

"Race! Race!" she shouted as her friend wobbled and giggled beneath her.

Soon, KC was shouting at Poppy. "Giddyup," she called as Poppy staggered around the yard with KC shouting directions.

Sam thought he'd escaped, but Marsha the Martian leapt onto his back and shouted, "Ye ha!"

Her friend was already chasing a terrified Theo around the yard.

"Poppy! KC! Save me!" Sam called wobbling towards the grass and landing in a heap with his Martian rider.

Soon riders and horses were changing in a mad-cap chaotic competition. Some riders were collecting balloons and popping them on their way to the finish line.

Sam had managed to escape with Theo, and the two were merrily kicking balloons into Sam's home-made goal.

Poppy and KC couldn't believe how much fun the riders were, and how friendly and welcoming they'd been.

Lara, the oldest rider, was showing Poppy and

KC how to tighten stirrups, using her best friend Amy as a model horse.

Another group of girls was practising a Hula Horse dance for the next day's celebrations. They were  chatting merrily away while making up colourful ribbon skirts with nylon and elastic.

The day's festivities rolled happily on while KC's mum, Ruth and Kim were attending the horses out in the fields. In the late afternoon, Lara organized a procession of food carriers.

"You're Ant Number One," she said to KC. "Then you, then you," she continued, pointing at all the girls hanging around the tack room door.

With the marquee full to bursting, Poppy, KC and Sam sat around on camping chairs and upturned wooden boxes, chatting and planning games for the weekend.

Soon, Kim, Ruth and KC's mum were leading the ponies back to their stables. The party-goers waved as the line of horses marched dutifully into their stalls.

Finally, the last to return in from the fields was Phoebe. She came around the corner with Dixie trotting happily behind her.

"It's Dixie!" shouted Poppy and KC in unison. They raced up to Phoebe and Dixie with Marsha and Lara.

"Any luck with Dixie today?" asked Lara.

Phoebe looked really down. "No, we've been trying him out in the field, but the saddling is still causing a problem," said Phoebe.

"Come on Pheebs," said Lara. "It's early days yet. Don't get so down."

"It's all right for you," Phoebe snapped. "You're fine. It's me and Dixie that seem to be the problems around here."

Lara frowned. "Nobody says you're a problem, Pheebs," she said, quietly.

"It doesn't have to be said. It's pretty obvious," said Phoebe.

Lara looked shocked and slunk away, guiltily. Poppy and KC looked uncomfortable. "Um, do you fancy, um, coming swimming?" blurted KC.

Phoebe looked at KC as if she was mad. "Oh,

get lost," said Phoebe.

Phoebe clicked the horse on and marched him into the stable.

Poppy saw that her best friend was looking upset. "It's not you, you know. Phoebe's just upset about Dixie," putting her arm around KC.

"Let's go back to the party," she suggested.

Ten minutes later, Poppy and KC watched Phoebe limp angrily past the marquee. She was in her hooded zipper jacket and was carrying a small tack box.

Poppy jumped up to run after her but Lara grabbed her arm.

"Don't. She needs time," said Lara.

Poppy felt sad to see Phoebe walking home alone, without even a backward glance at the party. Poppy realised how lonely Phoebe must be.

It was dusk by the time the party finished. Poppy, KC and Sam had had the most incredible time. KC's mum was chatting happily with Ruth and Kim, so the three friends said goodnight and made their way back to the cabin.

The sky was mauve and pink as the sun slipped

down below the horizon. "I think the people here are really friendly, after all," KC sighed, happily.

"Yes," agreed Sam. "Theo's bringing his Robot raider game to the stables for me to try out."

Just as the three friends had cleared the stile to the horse meadow, they noticed someone in the field with Prince.

"Don't look now, but that Harriet girl's in the field," said Poppy.

KC strained to see over the hedge. "No, it can't be her," she said. "That person's much taller than Harriet – look!"

In the half-light it was hard for Poppy and Sam to make out the shapes, but KC was right. Whoever it was in the field with Prince was not Harriet. The stranger was taller, very thin and was wearing a hooded jacket.

"Well, I'm not interested," said Poppy. "It'll only be her rich father or something."

The three carried on to the cabin without giving the stranger a second thought.

Chapter 8

Showdown

The following morning, everyone in the cabin was woken from their sleep by someone hammering frantically on the door.

"All right, all right," said KC's mum, running. "What's the rush?"

When she opened the door, Lara and Marsha were panting breathlessly and looked flushed and very upset.

"There's trouble up at the stables," blurted Lara, urgently.

Poppy, KC and Sam were standing behind KC's mum within a second.

"It isn't Dixie, is it?"asked Poppy, anxiously.

"No, no," said Marsha. "It's the stables."

"Calm down, Marsha," said KC's mum. "I'll go get my medical bag."

"No, you don't understand – it's not that. Harriet Durston's tack was destroyed last night and somebody painted horrible things on her horse's shelter. She's accused Phoebe. She says she was seen in the field with Prince and unless Phoebe is banned from Rocky Mountain, she's going to get her father to close the stables down," cried Lara, without stopping to take a breath.

"OK, OK . . . Lara," said KC's mum. "Perhaps there's been a mistake. Hold on and I'll get my things and come up with you."

Poppy, KC and Sam looked knowingly at one another.

Poppy was upset; upset for Phoebe, not for Harriet Durston. Poppy knew that Harriet Durston was the kind of girl who courted bad feeling. Poppy also guessed that, although it was wrong to damage someone's property she imagined that Harriet had probably upset lots of people who might think of some way to get even.

Poppy raced off to the bedroom to get dressed, with KC squeezing through the door at the same time. KC closed the door behind them.

"What are we going to do?" she asked, urgently. "Supposing someone asks us if we saw anything? We can't lie and say we didn't see Phoebe in the field last night. I feel so bad. I feel really rotten."

"We can't be sure it was Phoebe," said Poppy, quickly.

"No, but she fits the description perfectly, Poppy," said KC. "Whoever it was in the field was Phoebe's height, wearing the same kind of jacket and Phoebe left on her own, ages before we did. For some reason, she went home the way we go back to our cabin – in the same direction as Prince's field."

Poppy thought for a moment. "Phoebe doesn't live near the cabins. Lara said she lives in town."

Poppy's head was spinning. She couldn't understand it. It just didn't make sense. Why would Phoebe pick on Harriet Durston when she was angry with Lara and the other girls at the stables? And, why would Phoebe take that way home, near Prince's field, in front of everyone, if she was planning to damage Harriet's tack?

"I don't think Phoebe did it," said Poppy. "It just doesn't make sense."

There was a sudden hammering on the door of their cabin. "Come on, you two, everyone's gone already," called Sam.

When the three friends got to the stables, Kim, Ruth and KC's mum were still trying to calm Harriet Durston down.

"I want her out of here," shrieked Harriet Durston, pointing her finger at Phoebe.

Phoebe was obviously in shock. Kim was standing with her arm around Phoebe's shoulder, trying to comfort her.

"It's no good accusing people without proof," said Ruth, sharply, to Harriet Durston. "It could have been anyone."

"It was her. She was seen. Someone told me. I've got a witness," said Harriet, smugly.

Phoebe was shaking with anger. "It's a lie. I wouldn't do that. I just wouldn't," said Phoebe, fighting back tears.

"Yes, you would. I see you watch me riding Prince. I see you spying on me. You're jealous of me," said Harriet.

"I think we've heard enough," said KC's mum,

calmly. "If there's been damage to property we need to call in the police and let them get to the bottom of it."

"If you don't get her off this land, then I'll make sure my father gets you all off. Horrible things she wrote on my shelter, horrible," shouted Harriet.

"Come on Harriet, I'll drive you home," said Ruth, gently taking Harriet's arm.

Harriet drew her arm away. "Then take me home now," she commanded.

Ruth gave a look of disapproval as she began to lead Harriet to her car.

Phoebe limped over to the tack room and took her jacket from the hook.

"I'll walk back with you," said Lara quietly to Phoebe.

"No – no thanks. I want to be on my own," said Phoebe, tearfully.

The small groups of onlookers moved silently from the stable yard.

"It's all my fault," said Kim to KC's mum. "I should have kept a closer eye on Phoebe. I knew that she was upset but never thought she'd do anything like this."

"Come on, you need a strong coffee," said KC's mum, leading Kim to the house.

Poppy, KC and Sam sat silently in the yard.

Dixie suddenly popped his head over the top of his stable door.

It was as if Dixie knew that something was going to happen, something sad and frightening. Sam thought for a moment then wandered over to Dixie's stable.

He hopped onto the door and patted Dixie's nose. "Who's a good boy?" whispered Sam, reassuringly.

Dixie snorted and shook his head happily. The boy and the pony seemed to share a quiet moment of friendship. "Maybe," Sam thought. "Maybe real ponies have got some kind of magic, after all. Maybe more than my 3D game ones."

Moments later, KC and Poppy were up on the stable door beside Sam.

"Come on," said Poppy. "We've got some investigating to do."

Feeling more inspired than ever, Poppy, KC and

Sam hurried down to Harriet's field, where Prince was grazing.

"Supposing Harriet or the police come and catch us round Prince and the shelter?" said KC, nervously.

"We'll think of something to tell them," replied Poppy, confidently.

KC and Sam always knew when Poppy meant business and today there was no mistaking the determination on her face.

Prince came racing up to Poppy and KC. Sam dived behind Poppy for protection. KC gave Prince a welcoming pat, then joined Poppy and Sam to search for clues around the horse's shelter.

There was no doubt that whoever had been in the shelter the night before had been intent on causing as much damage as possible. Harriet's saddle was covered in burnt stains from what looked and smelt like pure bleach being poured over it.

Prince's reins had been sliced right through with a razor sharp tool and horrible graffiti had been painted all over the inside of the shelter, saying "DURSTON OUT!"

"It's horrible," said Poppy gazing in dismay at the damage. "I mean, I don't like Harriet Durston but this is pretty scary."

"Look, what's that?" asked Poppy, seeing something sparkling in the dewy grass.

The three friends peered at the object.

"It's a key," blurted Sam.

 Poppy reached down and picked it up. The three friends inspected it and came to the conclusion that it was a modern steel key. It had no name but something had been scratched into the steel.

"Look," said Sam, noticing that there was a word engraved on the side of it.

Poppy tilted the key back and forth in the morning sunshine trying to read the markings.

"I can just make out one letter. Look – it's a 'P'," said Poppy.

"And, look," added Sam. "That letter near the end; it looks like an 'E'."

KC looked at the ground around the key.

"Uh oh," she said warily. "This doesn't look good."

KC had found some tracks but they were unusual. One was a clear footprint but the other print looked like it had been dragged along the muddy ground.

"Oh, Phoebe," said KC. "Only she could leave marks like this. Who else would leave this kind of print in the ground?"

Poppy and Sam had to agree. The indents left in the ground looked like someone had half walked and half dragged his or her foot.

Poppy felt really upset and disappointed and KC wished she hadn't found the print.

"So, that's it. It was Phoebe," said Sam.

Poppy put the key into her jacket pocket.

"We can't be sure it was Phoebe," she said, knowing that the evidence was too good to ignore.

"I think it's so sad. Phoebe's going to be banned from the stables and now Dixie will have no one and he'll be sold, probably to some child like Harriet Durston," said KC.

Poppy stood up and looked around. "The more

I see, the less I like," she said, sadly.

"Well, we should at least take the key back to Phoebe and try to get her to talk to us about it all. It's obviously Phoebe's key – it has a 'P' and an 'E' engraved on it. The key's bound to be needed to open something important," said Poppy, quickly.

"Maybe it was all just some kind of accident," KC mumbled, hopefully.

"Well, Phoebe must have struggled with the bleach because she's spilt it all over the ground," said Sam, holding his nose and pointing to white patches of burnt grass and bleached earth.

They followed the trail of bleach. It led out of the field and onto the pavement.

"I think if we follow these marks, they'll lead us straight to Phoebe's door," said KC, sadly.

Poppy, KC and Sam walked unenthusiastically out of the field following any markings they could see on the path. The trail became less and less easy to pick up the further they went from the paddock. Eventually, it led the three friends to a pretty avenue lined with trees and greenery.

"There!" exclaimed Sam. There were traces of

a white print in the grass and another drag mark right behind. It stopped at the gate entrance to a small modern house in the avenue.

Poppy took the key from her pocket and held it up.

"Ready?" she asked Sam and KC.

"Ready," they replied, taking deep breaths.

The three friends walked quietly up to the front door and knocked. There was no answer.

Poppy braced herself and knocked harder.

A young boy cycled up and leaned on his bike against the low hedge of the empty house.

"No one's in," he said helpfully, "I saw Phoebe and her folks go out in the car."

"Oh, thank you. Are you a neighbour?" asked Poppy, quickly.

"Yes, I live over there," said the boy, pointing to the house opposite Phoebe's.

"If you see Phoebe, can you tell her that her friends have got her key and would like to return it to her?" said Poppy.

"Sure, no problem," said the boy and with that he swung his bike around and shot away.

Chapter 9
The Discovery

On their way back to the stables, Poppy felt uneasy. She tried to imagine Phoebe tipping bleach over Harriet's saddle and tack, and she wondered just how Phoebe could have climbed up and painted all the horrible graffiti on Prince's shelter.

It just didn't make sense.

"You're scrunching again," said Sam. Sometimes, when Poppy was deep in thought, she scrunched up her nose and frowned intently.

Poppy laughed.

"Yes, you've definitely got gears clanking in your head," KC chuckled.

"Well, something's wrong and I can't put my finger on it," said Poppy.

"Wishful thinking, maybe," said Sam. "We all like Phoebe more than Harriet. So, we don't want Phoebe to be the one who's in trouble."

Poppy was sometimes surprised at how her younger brother of seven-and-a-half could be so thoughtful and mature.

"Yes, I suppose that's part of it, Sam," said Poppy. "But Phoebe doesn't seem like a stupid person to me. I'm sure she would have realised that she'd put everyone at the stables under suspicion and that she'd be found out in the end. And – doing something like that wouldn't help Dixie at all. If anything, it would make matters worse."

"People do strange things when they're upset," said KC.

Poppy shrugged. "Maybe," she said. "Anyway, we'll go back over to see Phoebe this afternoon. She might be back home by then and, hopefully, she'll tell us what happened."

For the rest of the day, between peanut butter sandwiches and leftover birthday cake, Sam was on the internet looking up information on ponies. He was determined to discover what was wrong with Dixie on the 'Your Horse and Pony Agony Aunt' website.

"Why do these help pages always have agony

Aunts?" mumbled Sam. "I bet there are lots of clever Agony Uncles, too, who know about horses and growing up and plants."

"Never mind, Sam," said Poppy. "Maybe when you leave school you'll be the first Agony Uncle."

"No, thanks," said Sam. "I'm going to be a top detective."

Poppy smiled.

"Did you know that if a horse keeps nodding its head in the stable, if you put a mirror in for it to look at, it stops doing it?" said Sam, smartly.

"Wow, that's clever," said KC.

"What about a horse that won't be ridden, like Dixie; is there anything about that?" asked Poppy.

"Bucking, rearing, not boxing, bolting – everything and anything, but nothing about lying on the ground and going on saddle-strike," said Sam, cheerfully.

"Keep looking Sam, you're bound to turn something up soon," said KC, brightly.

Poppy and KC were studying a local map. They had found Rocky Mountain stables, and Phoebe's house, and were marking another route to get them in and out of Bay Tree Farm.

"It has to be hound proof," demanded KC nervously. "Next time I might not outrun those vicious dogs."

"Of course you will," said Poppy. "But if all goes to plan, Nathan says we won't have to because, when we meet him tomorrow, he's going to bring some irresistible doggy treats."

"Well, they'd better be tasty," said KC. "And I mean more tasty than my leg."

When KC's mum returned to the cabin later that day, she looked tired and upset. KC knew that her mum wanted some space and quiet; KC could see by the way her mum moved around the room.

Sam stayed focused on his computer and the girls quietly carried on with their plans for photographing the sick pony at Bay Tree Farm.

KC's mum quietly brewed a cup of tea, sat down with her feet up on the small stool and sighed.

Poppy and KC could tell that things had not gone well at the stables between Kim and Harriet Duston's father but they didn't like to ask what had happened.

Suddenly Poppy realised the time. "We've got a key to return," she said, nudging KC.

"Yes, Phoebe's bound to be back now," said KC, calling to Sam.

The friends jumped up and put on their jackets.

"We'll be back soon, Mum. We're just going to see Phoebe," whispered KC.

"Don't be back too late – come back before it starts to get dark, please."

Poppy, KC and Sam tiptoed out of the cabin door and made their way along the woodland track.

"It's only a ten minute walk to Phoebe's from the paddock," said Poppy, "I haven't even decided what I'm going to say to her."

KC frowned, "I'd like to say sorry, but I don't know what for," she said.

"We'll just give her the key and get back home," said Sam. "I'm sure I can find out why Dixie's acting strangely. There are loads of sites with horsey info."

"Don't worry, Sam, we'll get back to your computer as soon as we can," grinned Poppy.

They were just approaching Prince's paddock from the other field, when Poppy saw a figure next to Prince's shelter.

"Wait!" she whispered to the others, "It looks like Harriet's around."

KC and Sam peered silently over the hedge.

"That's the person we saw last night!" exclaimed KC. "It's the same jacket with the hood up, and they're skinny, and it looks like they're the same height, too."

The three watched the stranger move around the paddock. Suddenly, the figure dropped down and felt through the long grass.

"What are they doing?" mused KC puzzled.

Poppy gasped. "I know," she whispered urgently. "They're looking for this."

Poppy held the key up in the afternoon light.

The three were surprised and wary of their discovery.

"If it's Phoebe, let's just march up to her and confront her," said KC, bravely.

"Yes," whispered Poppy. "But supposing, just supposing, it's someone else?"

Poppy took a deep breath. "We're going to creep into the paddock and give the key back. But before we do, we're going to make sure we know exactly who it is," she said.

KC felt her skin prickle.

"Come on," said Poppy. "Remember: act like a tiger, creep like a cat."

The three figures moved silently just below the top of the bushy hedge. When they reached the stone step, Sam was the first to crawl over on his hands and knees. He felt invisible and brave, like a real adventurer.

The three moved along the grass on their bellies. The figure was still rustling about in the grass, frantically searching. Prince kept nuzzling the hooded stranger on the back for attention but the person kept pushing Prince away irritably.

Suddenly Prince's ears pricked up. The pony sensed there were three spies moving about in the grass. Prince's nostrils flared excitedly. He recognised KC and Poppy's scent in an instant. Suddenly, he was galloping happily over to them at breakneck speed.

Poppy and KC put their heads down tight to the ground but Sam looked up in horror at the biggest, whitest, fastest horse he'd ever seen, come thundering towards him.

Within the blink of an eye, Sam's courage flooded away. He was on his feet, waving his arms frantically in the air and racing back to the hedge.

"Help," cried Sam, in terror. "It's a charge!" Sam's bright blue eyes were wide with fear.

Hearing all the commotion, the stranger stayed as still as a statue for a moment, in shock.

Prince was already beside KC, sticking his long nose under her belly and trying desperately to get her to stand up and fuss over him.

KC gently tapped Prince's nose, half giggling and shrieking, "Go away, Prince."

But it was too late. The stranger leapt up and raced towards the other exit of the paddock.

"Come on, they're getting away," cried Poppy belting through the grass.

KC jumped to her feet dragging Sam out from under the hedge. "Come on, silly, we've got to catch them," she said.

Chapter 10

The Chase

Poppy was already at the far end of the paddock with Sam and KC close behind.

Prince was enjoying all the excitement and was running around in circles neighing happily and kicking up dust.

Sam and KC could see Poppy charging along the street ahead. The hooded figure was some way in front of her. As Poppy tore on after the stranger, she suddenly realised that she could not be chasing Phoebe, because this person could run like the wind and had no problem jumping over fences.

Poppy knew the culprit had to be caught; it was the only way to save Phoebe, and Dixie, too.

As the stranger turned into the avenue, Poppy's heart was pounding. The stranger was heading straight for Phoebe's house.

Poppy just couldn't figure it out. Poppy raced up to Phoebe's front gate just in time to see the stranger leap onto a tall picnic table at the end of the garden and reach up to the back garden wall.

"Quick," Poppy shouted to KC and Sam. "They're getting away."

The stranger stood on the wall for a second and glanced sideways at Poppy from inside the hood.

Then the figure disappeared over the wall, and down to the other side.

Poppy was hopping on the spot when Sam and KC reached her.

"We have to go over the wall," she said, urgently.

"Come on," said Sam, darting through the garden and hopping onto the picnic table.

Sam stood high up on the wall and looked down through the streets.

Suddenly, he spotted the hooded figure running up another street.

"I've seen them, come on," he called as Poppy and KC landed softly on the ground on the other side.

Sam leapt down and raced towards the street where he had seen the stranger dash.

All three were now bravely surging ahead, determined not to lose their suspect. They charged around the corner just in time to see the hooded figure disappear over another high stone wall. They raced up to it but it was too high for them to reach. The stranger had obviously used a green dustbin standing nearby as a step.

One by one, they clambered onto the bin and pulled themselves onto the wall. They jumped down the other side and suddenly found themselves standing in someone's garden at the back of a small house.

Poppy stood and gazed around. She had a strange feeling she had been there before.

Suddenly there was a loud clatter and a clang. Sam was groaning and hobbling around in pain.

He had stepped forward and tripped on a stack of paint tins and a steel ladder.

Suddenly, the back door flew open and a familiar face peered out.

"Who's there?" called a man's voice.

Poppy, KC and Sam couldn't believe their eyes.

They had somehow arrived in Nathan's small back garden and it was Nathan's father who was calling out to them

"Sorry . . . it's . . . it's us," Poppy called in a small, breathless voice.

"Who's us?" demanded Nathan's dad, impatiently.

"I know who it is. It's my friends," piped Kylie's bright little voice.

A moment later, Kylie was upon the group and dragging KC and Poppy in by the hand with Sam hobbling in behind them.

"Hello kids," said Nathan's dad, in a warm voice, "You chose the hard way in didn't you? But I'm afraid Nathan's not in."

Kylie pulled on Poppy's jacket. "Daddy says Nat's in the dog-house 'cause he lost the paint box key."

Poppy, KC and Sam couldn't believe their ears.

Poppy's head spun in confusion. Sam's face fell in shock.

"Kylie, that's not for you to talk about," said her dad, gently.

Poppy fumbled in her jacket pocket and held out the steel key they had found at the paddock.

"Is this the key to your paint box?" said Poppy, anxiously.

"Yes!" exclaimed Nathan's dad, taking it from Poppy as if it were treasure.

They heard the sound of someone panting and approaching them all from the entrance hall.

The kitchen door creaked open and Nathan stepped in, breathlessly.

"Look what your friends have found!" exclaimed his dad, happily.

His dad waved the key triumphantly in the air.

Nathan looked at everyone in total horror.

"Where did you find it?" Nathan asked Poppy, in a trembling voice.

"Where you left it," said Poppy.

Nathan walked up to a chair and collapsed into it. Tears began to flood into his eyes.

"You don't understand," cried Nathan. "Harriet Durston's father had my dad dumped out of his workshop. He had Dad thrown off that land so that she could have it for nothing but a stupid horse."

Sam stepped up to Nathan. "But Nathan, what you did there was pretty mean. Making Phoebe take the blame for causing all that damage," he said, disappointed.

"Phoebe? Phoebe's taken the blame?" asked Nathan, shocked. "Honestly, I didn't know that would happen. I always use Phoebe's garden as a short cut from the adventure playground. I didn't think she'd get the blame for it," cried Nathan.

"What damage?" asked Nathan's dad, anxiously.

"I, I destroyed Harriet Duston's riding kit," said Nathan, quietly.

"You did what?" asked his dad, shocked.

Nathan's face flushed red and he tried to fight

back his tears. "And I painted graffiti on the horse's shelter," he whispered.

Nathan's dad put his hand on Nathan's shoulder. "Sounds to me like you've done something silly; something that someone else is getting blamed for."

As tears streamed down Nathan's face he nodded, shamefaced. "I was angry, Dad. Durston kept bothering you and telling you he wanted the land where you had your workshop. I heard you arguing on the phone. I know what he did. He had someone in the council get you thrown out of that paddock. He's destroyed your business," gasped Nathan.

"I'm old enough to fight my own battles, Nathan. I'd already put in an appeal. People are looking into what might be some strange dealings. And, anyway, I decided I'd look for another workshop, one that's closer to Kylie's school," said Nathan's dad, sternly.

"The footprints; I don't understand. Why did you leave those strange markings on the ground?" asked Poppy.

Nathan thought for a moment then realised what had happened.

"It must have been this," he said. He got up from the chair, went outside and rummaged around the back of greenhouse.

When he returned he was dragging something behind him. It was a heavy canvas bag which was long like a tent bag and filled to the brim with heavy tools. The end of the bag was scraping across the floor. Nathan half lifted and dragged it onto the kitchen table.

"I found the rest of Dad's tools at the back of Harriet Duston's horse shelter. Durston had taken them from Dad's workshop and hidden them there," said Nathan.

"Naughty, naughty" said Kylie doing her new fairy dance for everyone to admire.

Nathan's dad smiled. "You got my carpentry tools back," he said, proudly. "That's great."

Nathan nodded.

"However, it doesn't excuse you destroying

other people's property. I think we'd better go up to the stables this evening and straighten things out," he said. "Looks like you're going to be paying Harriet most of your allowance for a while; a saddle costs a lot."

"I'm sorry," Nathan said to Sam, Poppy and KC.

Sam shrugged, uncomfortably. "Yes, well," he said.

"We need to let Phoebe know that everything's going to be OK," said Poppy, quickly. "Harriet Durston is demanding that Phoebe is banned from Rocky Mountain stables. She said she has a witness who saw Phoebe cause all the damage."

Nathan put his head in his hands. "It's all a lie. I did it," he said, quietly, "I'm really sorry, but it was me."

"Harriet Durston's a liar," said KC, angrily.

"Well, she's not going to get away with it, is she?" asked Nathan.

"Thank you for bringing all this out into the open," said Nathan's dad to the friends. "It's good for me and good for Nathan, too. We can sort this mess out together."

Poppy, Sam and KC walked back down the road with Nathan and his dad. They said goodbye when they arrived at Phoebe's gate.

Nathan was ready to tell Phoebe and her family everything.

When Poppy, Sam and KC got back to the cabin, KC's mum woke up with a start. She sat up straight and rubbed her tired eyes.

"I must have fallen asleep," she said, groggily, "What have you three been up to?"

"Oh, not much," said KC impishly. "Just the usual detective stuff."

The three friends laughed.

"Come on. We've got a busy day tomorrow. We're going to take some very important photographs," said Poppy, enthusiastically.

Chapter 11
All in a Picture

By early next morning, Sam had managed to upload the photographs of the strange man locking the pony into the Bay Tree Farm stable onto the computer. He'd also got a good shot of the vehicle and the number plate, too.

"These are great," said Poppy, excitedly.

"It's easy when you know how," Sam shrugged.

"Well, they're really clear, Sam," agreed KC. "Now all we need to do is get a picture of that poor pony to give to mum and Ruth as evidence."

Poppy had already packed things ready for their trip to Bay Tree Farm. KC was wearing three pairs of socks and had borrowed Sam's shin pads.

"You'll never be able to run in all that!" laughed Poppy.

KC proudly put her leg up on the chair. "Not even the Hounds of Baskervilles could bite through this," she said proudly. "So it doesn't matter how slowly I run."

Sam rolled his eyes and looked up at the ceiling. "Well, I don't think we're going to get very far without Nathan's magic dog food," he said.

"Nathan's grounded," said Poppy. "So we'll just have to manage without his magic dog food. Anyway, the dogs might not even be there."

"Whatever," shrugged Sam. "I still think we should have told KC's mum or Ruth about the pony at Bay Tree."

"Sam, the pony might not even be there anymore, and who's going to believe us unless we have proof?" asked Poppy.

"Right! That's where you come in. Have you got your camera, Sam?" prompted KC, efficiently.

Sam nodded and tapped his rucksack.

"If we go back to Bay Tree farm to find out what's happened to that poor pony, I have a strange feeling we'll also discover what's been troubling Dixie," said Poppy.

"I hope so," said KC. "Phoebe might be off the hook with Harriet Durston but it's going to break her heart if Dixie leaves the stables."

The three detectives headed out across the meadow towards Rocky Mountain stables. Now that Poppy had a map of the area, they were confident they'd find a good way to Bay Tree Farm without Nathan's help.

When they arrived at Rocky Mountain, Marsha the Martian was sitting on her little black pony waiting for the rest of the riders to join her for a hack. She gave Poppy, Sam and KC a happy wave.

Suddenly, Phoebe appeared from Dixie's stable. Her cheeks were flushed pink as she hurried over to the group as fast as she could.

"Wait!" she called. "I need to talk to you."

The three friends stopped and walked towards Dixie's stable. Phoebe looked slightly embarrassed but she was much calmer and even a little brighter than the last time they'd seen her.

"Nathan and his dad came to see me last night. They told me everything about Durston and Nathan's dad's workshop and . . . I feel very bad for Nathan but I just wanted to say thanks. If it hadn't been for you three, no one would have known the truth." Phoebe gave a faint smile. "What you did has saved me from a ban at the stables. I couldn't stay away from Dixie, it would be terrible."

"That horrible Harriet, she can't just go around accusing people of things," said Poppy.

Suddenly, the three heard a familiar sound. They turned to see a battered car drive past the stable yard and off down the lane.

"There goes trouble," said Phoebe, her sharp eyes burning at the two people sitting in the front of the car.

Poppy's eyes widened with surprise when she saw who was in the car. She was sure the man driving was the same man they had seen at Bay Tree Farm. Even though the car wasn't pulling a trailer, the sound and the look of the car was very easy to remember.

KC nudged Poppy. "Did you see that? That was the car we saw at Bay Tree Farm. I'm sure it is. The number plate was the same!" she said excitedly.

"Who was that?" Sam asked Phoebe, puzzled.

"Trouble, that's who," said Phoebe darkly. "That was Harriet Durston and her father. What a horrible pair."

"Mr Durston? Are you saying that was Mr Durston?" said Poppy, her eyes twinkling with excitement.

"Yes. Looks like Kim's just sent them packing. They came up shouting about the damage I'd caused to Harriet Durston's horse shelter and demanded that Kim send me back home. But now that Nathan's owned up to it, Kim's told them to get lost," said Phoebe, looking overjoyed.

Poppy, Sam and KC exchanged knowing looks. Poppy realised that if Mr. Durston was the cruel man they had seen unloading the battered horse at Bay Tree Farm, then it was even more important that they get the photographs they needed of the sick pony. If they could prove that Mr. Durston abused his animals, then they could finally find out what had happened to poor Dixie.

"Um, we've got to go," said KC, now desperate to get to Bay Tree Farm. "But do you want to come swimming with us later this week?"

Phoebe beamed with surprise. "I'd love to," she said, happily.

"Great, see you later!" called Poppy, as the three friends dashed off to find their evidence at Bay Tree Farm.

They decided they would approach Bay Tree from the hillside where the camels were grazing. There was a stile they could climb over to escape. It was far closer to the barns than either racing down the front track or back through the paddock with the copse at the end.

Poppy, KC and Sam were very nervous.

"Somehow, we have to get into that barn and photograph the pony before the hounds sniff us," said Poppy.

"I think the nutmeg will help," Sam commented. He had read a story about a convict who had escaped from police hounds by covering himself in nutmeg powder. Apparently the police hounds had hated the smell of the spice so much that they refused to follow it.

KC sniffed her sleeve. "Phew, it is strong," she said with a loud sneeze.

Sam checked in his kit to make sure he'd remembered the torch.

He knew that his camera's flash would not be strong enough for a clear picture of the pony in such a dark barn.

The three took a shortcut through the park and over the little bridge. But, instead of heading out onto the main road in the direction Nathan had taken them earlier, they followed a route Poppy had mapped out that took them around the back fields.

After a long walk, the three detectives found themselves standing on the hilltop, gazing down at a small contented herd of alpacas.

"I thought they were camels," said KC.

"Well, almost," said Poppy.

"I bet they're as smelly as camels," said Sam.

The alpacas were all sizes and colours, from jet black to the fluffiest cream. KC thought they were funny looking. They had the biggest eyes she'd ever seen, cute little fringes, and they were draped in the fluffiest hair she'd ever seen.

The animals craned their long necks timidly to sniff at the group. Sam kept a safe distance from the herd but was clicking his camera from all angles, just like a tourist.

Suddenly, they heard a noise that made their hearts miss a beat. The hounds were loose and they had the friends in their sights.

"Run!" shouted Sam, blasting back up the hillside.

KC stood for a moment and froze. Then she looked at her leg shields. Somehow they didn't seem so cool, strong and safe, now that the hounds were making their way at speed towards them.

"Wait for me," she yelled.

She tried lifting her legs and racing upwards but they felt so heavy that she thought she was going to fall backwards. She quickly turned back to see the mighty Great Danes clearing the stile and realised that they were now only a few yards away.

KC turned back to start running but her foot caught on a grassy mound. It sent her straight over onto her back.

Poppy and Sam looked back in dread. Bravely, they turned and raced back to help KC. They couldn't leave her to the hounds.

Sam had his kit bag ready to strike at the dogs. "Don't worry, KC," he cried, "They won't touch you with the nutmeg powder on."

As KC lay helpless on the grass, the face of a dribbling, dog loomed over her. KC couldn't believe the horror that was now facing her.

And then, instead of opening its jaws to bite, the mighty dog whined, wagged its tail and gave KC the biggest, sloppiest lick she'd ever had. Seconds later, the other dog had leapt onto Sam and was licking his face.

"Help, I can't breathe!" cried KC. "It's licking me to death."

A woman's voice cut through the shrieks. "Smudge, stop that this minute," she said, sharply.

One dog raced happily up to the woman. She patted it and told it to calm down as she walked quickly up to the three terror-struck faces.

KC was sneezing from the nutmeg spice and

wiping away the dog's slobber, all at once.

"Yuck," cried KC, disgusted, "I need a shower."

Meanwhile, Sam had found his feet and was saying in a small and trembling voice to the other dog, " Sit!" He was pointing out a trembling arm and trying to look masterful.

"Fudge!" shouted the woman, "Come here and behave yourself."

Poppy found herself standing beside the sick pony. She was relieved to see that Sam and KC were OK, but now she was looking worriedly at the woman who stood before them.

"I'm sorry my dogs scared you," said the woman, warmly, "They're really very friendly."

KC brushed herself down and Sam went to stand bravely beside Poppy.

"Are you both all right?" the woman asked KC and Sam.

"Uhhh, I've got slobber all over my camera lens," said Sam, slightly annoyed.

"I'm very sorry about that," said the woman. "You weren't here a few days ago, were you?" she continued. "When I got back from the market last week someone was here. Smudge and Fudge chased them away from the farm. Was it you?"

Poppy, KC and Sam looked guiltily at one another.

"Ah!" said the woman, "Looks like it was you."

"We never said that!" blurted Sam, trying to dry the lens on his jacket.

The woman smiled, "It's OK," she said, quickly "I often have children come over from town. They're always trying to ride my alpacas. It's not a good thing to do though."

"We didn't try to ride them," said Sam

"Well, no harm done," said the woman. "No one's ridden one yet. Alpacas won't be ridden. They're just not bred for it."

"They have strange bodies," said KC.

"My name's Amanda," said the woman. "When you were here, did you happen to see anyone leaving that pony?" she asked, pointing at the sick little pony. "They must have left him here when I was running my animal rescue stall at the market," said Amanda.

"It's not your pony?" asked Poppy.

"I'd never allow a pony to get into that condition. I'm an animal lover. Everyone knows that Amanda Price loves animals," she said. "I don't know where it came from but, if I ever find out, I'll have them on charges of neglect."

"Really?" said Poppy.

"Really!" said Amanda angrily. "I've sometimes taken the odd animal in as a rescue project, but I've never in my life seen anything as neglected or abused as that poor little pony. And, some awful person reported me to the RSPCA for neglect."

Poppy, KC and Sam suddenly sprang to life.

"But, but we've got pictures of the man who dumped the pony here. That's why we came back here, to get some pictures of the pony and report the man." Poppy was speaking so fast with excitement that Amanda could barely keep up.

"I've checked them on my computer. I've got them in my camera, too. Look!" said Sam, proudly holding up the camera.

"That's wonderful," exclaimed Amanda, with relief. "Are you sure the pictures are clear enough?"

Sam nodded confidently. "Yes," he said in his coolest voice.

"You just wait until I find who left that poor little creature here. I'll have them up before a judge before they can sneeze," scowled Amanda.

"We know who it was," said Poppy quickly. "At least – we think we do."

Fudge sniffed and snorted at KC's jacket.

"Fudge – leave that poor girl alone," commanded Amanda, "I'm really sorry but you seem to be wearing something he likes. What perfume is it?"

"Perfume? No, it's just nutmeg," said KC, blushing.

"Oh, they love nutmeg. They'll follow it anywhere. Nutmeg, ginger, cinnamon, they love spices," laughed Amanda.

Amanda reached out and shook hands with the three friends. KC gave Sam a frown and tried to brush off the nutmeg.

Sam shrugged innocently. "It was only in a story," he said before KC could reprimand him.

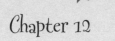

Chapter 12

Dixie on Show

Later that day, Poppy, KC and Sam arrived at Bay Tree Farm with KC's mum, Ruth and Kim. Amanda had learned from the three detectives all about Dixie going on saddle-strike, so she'd invited Kim to Bay Tree to see if she could help.

While Ruth and KC's mum gave the sick pony some vitamins and treatment, Poppy, KC, Sam and Kim talked to Amanda about Dixie's strange problem.

"The thing is," said Kim, "I can't keep Dixie at the stables. I can't afford to keep a horse that won't be ridden."

"Of course. I understand completely," said Amanda, "Dixie was a rescue pony. He's always been with me, since he was a tiny foal. I've never tried to ride him. He's just been happy grazing with the alpacas."

"But that doesn't explain why he behaves so strangely when we put a saddle on his back," said

Kim puzzled. "And I've got a girl at the stables who adores Dixie. It's going to be very hard for me to separate them now."

Amanda looked thoughtful. "I would take Dixie back and return your money, but it's hard running this place on my own. I'm trying to raise funds to create an official animal welfare centre here, so that I can help more animals," she said.

"That's wonderful," replied Kim "If only Dixie could be entered into competitions, then at least he'd earn his keep."

Poppy, KC and Sam were watching the alpacas grazing when suddenly Poppy leapt to her feet. She'd had an incredible idea. In fact, it was the best idea she'd ever had.

"I've got it!" she yelped. "I think I know what Dixie's problem is."

Sam and KC's eyes lit up.

"Watch!" said Poppy, excitedly.

Poppy walked quietly up to a small grazing alpaca. Talking gently to it, she held its strong long hair and hauled herself onto its back. Within a second the alpaca went down on its front legs, then its back legs and refused to budge an inch.

"That's it!" said KC's mum, amazed. "The alpacas have taught Dixie their strange habits. He thinks he's doing what he should be doing by lying down."

Sam laughed, "Dixie thinks he's an alpaca."

"Yes," said KC, "He's just copying the herd."

"How strange," said Amanda. "The town children are always sneaking into the field to try to ride the alpacas. Everyone knows an alpaca is not for riding. Dixie must have been copying the alpacas all this time and has grown up thinking it's normal behaviour to go down with something on his back."

Poppy, KC and Sam were overjoyed.

"It looks like you brought some pretty cool detectives with you," Ruth said to KC's mum.

KC's mum laughed, "I knew they'd probably solve the mystery in the end," she said, proudly.

The day before they were due to leave Rocky Mountain holiday centre, Kim invited everyone to the stables for a farewell get-together.

"We've got a double celebration," said Kim,

"Not only are we celebrating ten years of Rocky Mountain riding but, thanks to our three wonderful detectives, Mr Durston has been charged with neglect and other criminal dealings. The stables won't be bullied or threatened by him anymore."

Poppy, KC and Sam were filled with pride and satisfaction. "We've done it again, Poppy!" said KC as she put an arm around her best friend.

Just then, the crowd heard a clatter of hooves coming up the lane towards the stables. Everyone shrieked with delight as a pony and trap pulled into the stable courtyard.

Phoebe was sitting proudly at the reins of the carriage with Dixie brushed up and sparkling, at the head. Amanda hopped down from the passenger side and held out a small plastic bucket.

"We're collecting for Bay Tree Animal Centre, so

come on, throw in your change," she encouraged.

Coins were flying into the bucket as everyone crowded around Dixie and Phoebe.

"He looks fantastic," said Poppy, happily.

"Thanks," said Phoebe. "He still won't have a saddle on his back but," Phoebe gave a clever wink, "the neck collar is closer to the withers so he's perfectly comfortably with a free back and side reins. I think we're going to go places, Dixie and I. And we have the horse and carriage booked all through spring for weddings and parties."

"Amazing," said KC, patting Dixie with pride.

"Anyone for a ride?" called Phoebe.

Within a second, Sam was sitting beside her.

"You?" said Poppy in surprise. "Riding?"

"Whatever," said Sam. But his eyes lit up as Phoebe jigged the reins and they trotted away.

"Well, it looks like you girls have got some horse lessons to catch up on," said Kim, cheerfully.

"Wow, what a holiday: detectives one week, champion riders the next!" exclaimed Poppy.

"Yes, I think this adventure holiday is only just beginning," agreed KC, with delight.

If you've enjoyed meeting Poppy,
KC and Sam, you can try one of these
other exciting books in the
Three Together series.